The Tall Grass

Story by Cameron Macintosh
Illustrations by Rotem Teplow

Contents

Chapter 1

Sunshine in the Grass

This story takes place many years ago, in the 1800s.

Harriet, her papa and her little sister, Anna, lived on a farm in the country. Their farm was near a big field of tall grass.

Often, the weather was hot and dry. It was hard to grow potatoes in the family's vegetable garden.

The family had a cow called Sunshine.
They were lucky to have Sunshine.
She gave them milk each day.

Every morning, Harriet took a bucket of food from the barn to Sunshine's pen.

One morning, Harriet went from the barn to Sunshine's pen with a bucket of food. She unlocked the gate to the pen.

Suddenly, she heard Anna shouting from the vegetable garden.
"I've found some potatoes!" Anna cried.

Harriet ran over to help her.

The girls worked together, digging up the potatoes.

Just then, Harriet heard a sound coming from the field of tall grass.

"Oh, no!" Harriet cried loudly. "I can hear Sunshine in the grass. I left the gate open!"

"We must tell Papa," said Anna.

"Papa has gone on his horse to fix the fence
by the creek," said Harriet.
"We will have to find Sunshine ourselves."

"But if we walk into the tall grass,
we might get lost," said Anna.

Harriet stopped to think.

"I know what to do!" she said.
"I need to go to the barn.
You stay here in case Sunshine comes back out."

Chapter 2

Two Long Ropes

Harriet ran from the vegetable garden
to the barn.
She soon found two long ropes.

Harriet rushed back to Anna.

"Help me tie these ropes together," Harriet said.
"I'll go into the grass to find Sunshine.
I'll unroll the rope along the ground as I go.
Then, when I find Sunshine,
I'll follow the rope back to you."

The girls tied the two ropes together tightly to make one very long, strong rope.

Harriet took one end of the very long rope. “I’m ready to go now,” she said.

“I’ll stay here,” said Anna. “I won’t let go of the rope.”

Chapter 3

A Walk in the Tall Grass

Harriet stepped slowly into the wild grass.
It was so thick and tall
that she couldn't see very far ahead.

Harriet walked deeper into the grass.

“Are you all right, Harriet?” called Anna.

“Yes, but I’m running out of rope,” said Harriet. “I’ll have to stop soon.”

Suddenly, Harriet heard something moving.

She pushed the tall grass out of her way.
There, she saw Sunshine eating some of the grass.

"Hello, Sunshine!" said Harriet, laughing.

Harriet tied the end of the rope
around Sunshine's neck.
Then, she followed the rope along the ground,
back towards the farm.

Soon, Harriet and Sunshine stepped through
one last clump of grass, out into the open.

Harriet and Anna walked Sunshine back into her pen.

Harriet shut the gate very carefully. "You must only go walking in short grass from now on," she said to Sunshine, with a laugh.